From the **Disney** Archives

CHANTICLEER
and the
•FOX•

A CHAUCERIAN TALE
RETOLD BY

FULTON ROBERTS

ILLUSTRATED BY

MARC DAVIS

Disney
PRESS
NEW YORK

Chanticleer and the Fox
is published by Disney Press,
a subsidiary of The Walt Disney Company,
500 South Buena Vista Street, Burbank, California 91521.
The story and art herein are copyright © 1991 The Walt Disney Company.
No part of this book may be printed or reproduced
in any manner whatsoever,
whether mechanical or electronic,
without the written permission of the publisher.
The stories, characters or incidents
in this publication are entirely fictional.
Printed and bound in the United States of America.
Library of Congress Catalog Card Number: 91-71341

Published by Disney Press
114 Fifth Avenue
New York, New York 10011
ISBN 1-56282-022-2/1-56282-072-9 (Lib. Bdg.)
10 9 8 7 6 5 4 3 2 1

CHANTICLEER
and the
•FOX•

Once, in a little village deep in the rolling green hills, there lived a proud rooster named Chanticleer.

He was proud of his shining golden feathers.

He was proud of his jaunty black tail.

He was proud of his handsome red comb and wattles.

He was proud of his sharp yellow beak.

And he was very proud of his hearty rooster crow.

Every morning, Chanticleer strutted up and down in front of the mirror, combing out his feathers and warming up his voice. "Cock-a-doodle-doo! A fine rooster are you! Cock-a-doodle-dee! A fine rooster—that's me!" he crowed.

Then he hopped outside into the early morning.

"Cock-a-doodle-doo, cock-a-doodle-doo," he cried into the brightening sky. "Wake up, you lazy sun! Get out of bed, you sleepyhead!"

It is hard to believe, but that vain Chanticleer actually thought his crowing made the sun rise!

However, it is true that his crowing made the village rise.

All around his perch, shutters banged open as villagers greeted the new day.

"How clever I am," Chanticleer thought as he watched his little world rising with the sun. "What would this village do without me?"

Yes, the life of that little village did revolve around Chanticleer.

He was the favorite of all the hens.

Every morning, as they went about their errands, they clucked and cackled about Chanticleer.

"Cluck, cluck, cluck! Did you see how handsome Chanticleer looked today?"

"Cackle, cackle, cackle! That splendid tail, those flashing eyes!"

"Cluck, cluck, cluck! Did you see how quickly he made the sun rise this morning?"

"Cackle, cackle, cackle! His voice was stronger than ever!"

"Oh my, oh my, what would we do without Chanticleer?"

Every morning, Chanticleer strutted about the village square, basking in the hens' praise.

Then off he went to the studio of Maestro Caruso, voice teacher, for a spray of throat soother, just in case the morning's crowing had put a strain on his vocal cords.

"I take no chances with my voice," he said. "My work is too important. Why, the villagers depend on me to start the day."

As a matter of fact, the villagers depended so much on Chanticleer that they voted unanimously for him to be their mayor.

They soon learned they had made a big mistake.

I regret to tell you that, in a very short time, Mayor Chanticleer became—well—somewhat overbearing.

Every Friday, after his appointment with the maestro, he strutted to the henhouse to count the week's egg production. "More eggs, more eggs!" he crowed. The hens were forced to lay eggs from dawn to dusk.

Chanticleer even threatened to wake the sun earlier if the hens didn't meet his quota!

It wasn't long before he was very unpopular indeed.

But you have probably guessed that he was too conceited to notice.

Early one morning, a ne'er-do-well fox named Reynard came wandering into the same rolling green hills near Chanticleer's village.

He was a dreamer and a get-rich-quick schemer, a rascal who had never done an honest day's work in his life. But right now, he was between schemes, and hungry.

Suddenly, he heard Chanticleer's loud crow echoing from hill to hill.

"Dinner!" he exclaimed and set out to follow the sound.

He found the little village and hid in some bushes to watch and wait—and to plan.

In the afternoon, when the hens had put on their finery and were parading in the square, Reynard strolled into the village.

He was an easy talker, a sly flatterer, and he quickly struck up a conversation with one of the most beautiful hens.

"My, what lovely tail feathers you have, my dear lady," he said smoothly, peering out from under his parasol. "Won't you join me for a light meal in my summer cottage just beyond those hills?"

I am sorry to say that the foolish hen fell for his flattery. She was never seen in the village again.

The next day, Reynard took a stroll through the village at lunch-time. He quickly fell in with another beautiful hen.

"My, what long, silky eyelashes you have, my dear lady," he murmured, winking and grinning. "May I escort you on your errands today?"

They spent the afternoon at the milliner's shop, looking at the latest collection of hats.

Then, "My summer cottage is just beyond those hills," said Reynard. "Won't you join me for some tea and crumpets?"

I am sorry to say that this foolish hen accepted his invitation, too. She was never seen in the village again.

The next day, Reynard took a stroll through the village at break-fast time. He soon found yet another beautiful hen, who was enjoying the early morning sun at an outdoor café.

"My, what a perky beak you have, my dear lady," he purred, sliding into a chair at her table. "Allow me to treat you to a cup of cappuccino."

Reynard soon discovered he had chosen a very talkative hen, and it wasn't long before she told Reynard how Chanticleer had become the mayor of the village—and a tyrant.

"Why, he makes us work so hard there's hardly any time for fun anymore," sighed the hen. "Election day is next week, and yet we are afraid to choose another mayor, for without Chanticleer, the sun will not rise!"

"Tsk, tsk," murmured Reynard, "what a sad story. You have my sympathy, dear lady. And now, please excuse me. I have important work to do."

I am happy to say that Reynard was in such a hurry he did not invite this fortunate hen to go to his "summer cottage." She lived a long, happy life and had many grandchildren.

All day long, Reynard searched the green hills from cavern to den to ravine, rounding up a gang of scoundrels.

"This is the scheme of the century!" he boasted. "The whole village will be ours!"

As evening fell, he and his companions marched into the village—to announce Reynard's campaign for mayor!

All that week, Reynard paraded about the village, waving his cane to the beat of his campaign drum and shouting his slogan, "No work, all play."

Crowds followed him to his platform in the middle of the village square and Reynard entertained them all day long.

"Work, work, work!" he shouted. "If you vote for Chanticleer that's all you'll get. Work and more work. It's time for some fun around here. Fun, fun, fun! If you vote for Reynard, that's all you'll get. Fun and more fun!"

"Hooray for Reynard, hooray!" cheered the crowd. "Away with Chanticleer. Who cares if the sun never rises? We'll just play all night long!"

Chanticleer watched with amusement from his perch high above the village square. But do you think he was worried?

I regret to say you are right. Chanticleer was much too conceited to worry.

"What foolishness!" he snorted, shaking out his magnificent tail feathers. Then he went back inside to practice his crowing in front of the mirror.

Now when Chanticleer
strutted about the village
square, all he heard was
cackling and clucking
about Mr. Reynard.
"Did you hear my
crowing this morning?"
he asked one hen.
"I thought it was
particularly powerful."

"Cluck, cluck, cluck!"
she replied. "I stayed out
very late last night at
Mr. Reynard's carnival.
I heard your crowing just
as I came home. Then I
went straight to sleep!"

"How are things at the henhouse?" he asked four of the best egg layers.

"Cackle, cackle, cackle!" they replied. "We haven't been to the henhouse for days. We're having too much fun at Mr. Reynard's carnival!"

And now, as you have probably guessed, Chanticleer was beginning to worry!

But Reynard had still more mischief to make.

He turned up with the notorious Señor Poco Loco, the dashing, never-defeated dueling rooster, a friend from previous adventures.

And he introduced Poco Loco to Chanticleer's own beloved Mademoiselle Henrietta!

When Chanticleer came to call that very evening, Henrietta was on the way to Reynard's carnival with Señor Poco Loco!

And now Chanticleer was more than worried. He was angry.

I am sorry to say that his pride was so hurt that he challenged Señor Poco Loco—the undefeated Señor Poco Loco—to a duel at daybreak!

The entire village gathered at the village green at dawn.
   Señor Poco Loco cut a frightening figure, flexing his sword and glaring fiercely at Chanticleer.

At the other end of the green, Chanticleer looked small and helpless. He braced himself, heart pounding, legs shaking, nearly fainting with fear.

Reynard lounged on the sidelines, smiling smugly. Only last night, under cover of darkness, while the villagers played at the carnival, he and his cohorts had raided the henhouse in a pre-victory celebration. Soon the whole village would be his.

With a shout, the duel began.

Would you be surprised to learn that Chanticleer fought bravely? He was afraid, but he was not a coward.

The villagers were won over by Chanticleer's courage. They began to cheer him on. "Chanticleer, Chanticleer!" they shouted. But his courage was no match for Señor Poco Loco's superior skill at swordplay.

Soon the fight turned against him.

But Sergeant, the village police dog, had discovered the destruction of the henhouse.

Just as Poco Loco thrust Chanticleer to the ground, Sergeant burst through the crowd waving his billy club and making straight for Reynard.

The villagers grabbed for Reynard, but he slipped out of his cloak and ran off into the woods. Poco Loco took advantage of the confusion to fly off into the hills.

I am happy to say neither one ever came back to the village again.

Chanticleer threw down his sword, pulled on his waistcoat, and hurried to the henhouse.

"This is all my fault," he cried, tearing his clothes in dismay. "What a foolish rooster I have been!"

He was so ashamed he spent the next three days in bed. To everyone's surprise, the sun continued to rise, even without his crowing.

Yes, the sun did continue to rise. But the villagers did not. For Chanticleer's crowing had been their alarm clock.

At a meeting in the village hall, they decided to ask him to return to work.

Rico Rooster caught up with Chanticleer just as he was sneaking out of the village forever.

"How can I face anyone?" sighed Chanticleer. "I have been such a fool."

"Cheer up," said Rico. "We have all been fools. But we have all learned something from Mr. Reynard."

"What?" asked Chanticleer.

"No one in the village is more important than anyone else," said Rico. "Not even you, Chanticleer. Now we know that the sun gets up by itself. But we do not get up by ourselves. We still need you to wake us."

"You do?" asked Chanticleer, straightening up a bit and shaking out his feathers.

"Yes, we do," said Rico, "because we have learned another thing. We must work or our village will not run. We must work, but we need time to play also."

And he was right.

I am happy to tell you that Chanticleer decided to return to the village.

Every morning the sun rose, and Chanticleer crowed his magnificent crow to wake up the villagers.

But every afternoon, he crowed again at four o'clock—to tell everyone it was time to stop work and to start playing.

Now although he was not such a proud rooster, he was a much happier rooster.

But you have probably already guessed that!